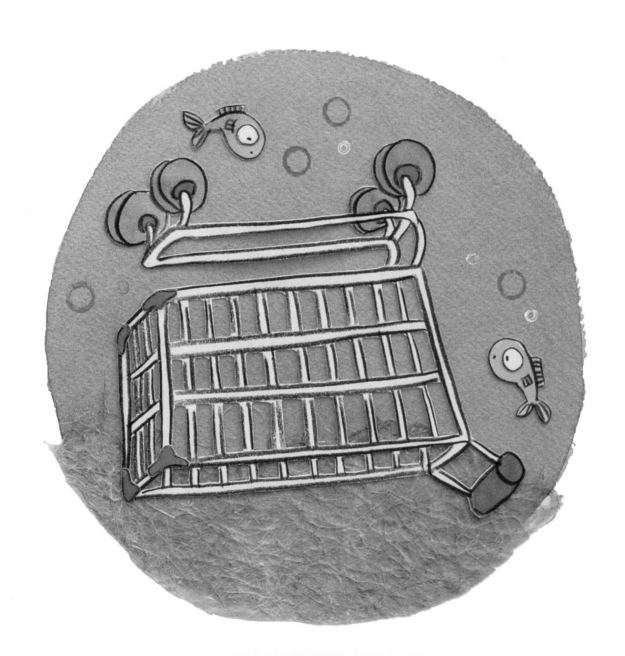

For Michael and Matt,
for being the penguins to my whale.

Special thanks to Mark Sholtez for recording and stitching together
my loose threads of musicianship.

First American Edition 2016
Kane Miller, A Division of EDC Publishing

Text and illustrations copyright © 2015 Peter Carnavas
First published in Australia by New Frontier Publishing
Translation rights arranged through Australian Licensing Corporation

For information contact:
Kane Miller, A Division of EDC Publishing
P.O. Box 470663
Tulsa, OK 74147-0663

www.kanemiller.com
www.edcpub.com
www.usbornebooksandmore.com

Library of Congress Control Number: 2015938651
Printed and bound in China
1 2 3 4 5 6 7 8 9 10
ISBN: 978-1-61067-458-4

BLUE WHALE
BLUES

PETER CARNAVAS

Kane Miller
A DIVISION OF EDC PUBLISHING

One blue morning, Penguin
heard Whale singing softly to
himself.

"Feeling blue, Whale?"
asked Penguin.

"Look at my bike," said Whale.
"I don't know which way it goes."

Penguin laughed.
"Oh, Whale," he said.
"Don't be blue. It's just upside down."

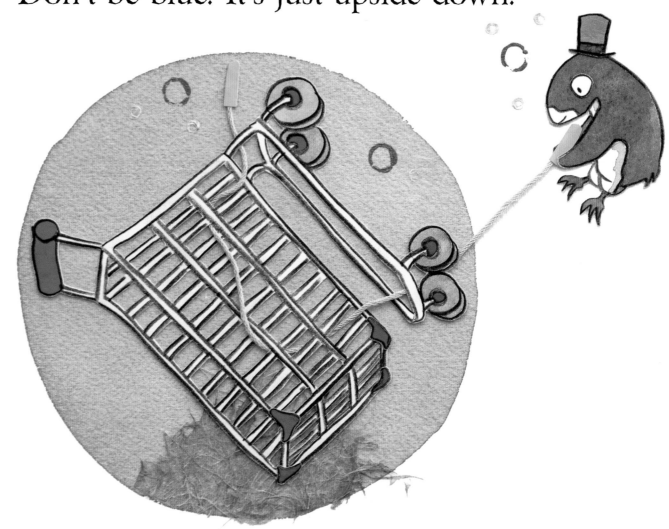

Whale felt much better.

But a short time later, Penguin heard Whale singing again.

"It's my bike again,"
said Whale.
"It's all wet."

Penguin laughed.
"Oh, Whale," he said.
"Don't be blue. You can use my towel."

Whale felt much better.

But later on, Penguin heard
Whale singing again.

"You look blue, Whale," said Penguin.

"It's my helmet
this time,"
said Whale.
"I don't know
where to put it."

Penguin laughed.
"Oh, Whale," he said. "Don't be blue.
Just put it on your nose."

Whale felt much better.

At last, everything was ready.

Whale and Penguin hopped on,
                   held on tight
                            and ...

nothing happened.

"Why aren't we moving?" said Whale.

Penguin wasn't listening.
He could see something strange
heading their way.

"What ... is ... that?" whispered Whale.
And Turtle said,

"It's a bike."

Whale slumped to the ocean floor.

"Um, Penguin," said Whale.
"I don't think my bike is a bike."

"I think you're right," said Penguin.

"And, Penguin," said Whale.
"I think you need legs to ride a bike.
I don't have any legs."

"I think you're right," said Penguin ...
and then ...

Penguin laughed
and this time,
so did Whale!

A BIG
  BLuE WHAlE
    BELly lAuGh!

HaHaHAHAha

Whale felt much,
MUCH better.

After that,
Whale forgot all about the bike

and he stopped feeling blue ...

even when
his guitar broke.